# OOPS

## ARTHUR GEISERT

Houghton Mifflin Company Boston 2006

Walter Lorraine Books

For our godchildren, Erin, Sasha, Cameron, Scott
—A.G. and B.G.

Walter Lorraine (wr) Books

*Library of Congress Cataloging-in-Publication Data*

Geisert, Arthur.
    Oops / Arthur Geisert.
      p. cm.
    "Walter Lorraine Books."
    Summary: Depicts, in wordless illustrations, how a little spilled
  milk led to the destruction of the pig family's house.
    ISBN-13: 978-0-618-60904-8
    ISBN-10: 0-618-60904-0
    [Pigs—Fiction.  2. Stories without words.]    I. Title.
  PZ7.G2724Oo 2006
  [E]—dc22
                                                      2005030850


Printed in Malaysia
TWP  10  9  8  7  6  5  4  3  2  1

# OOPS

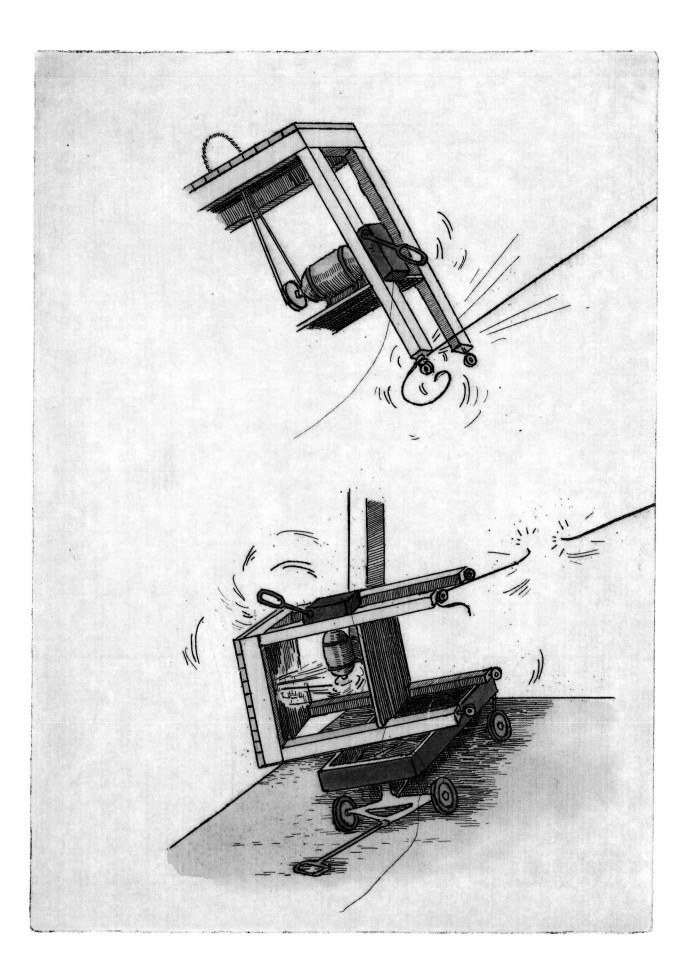

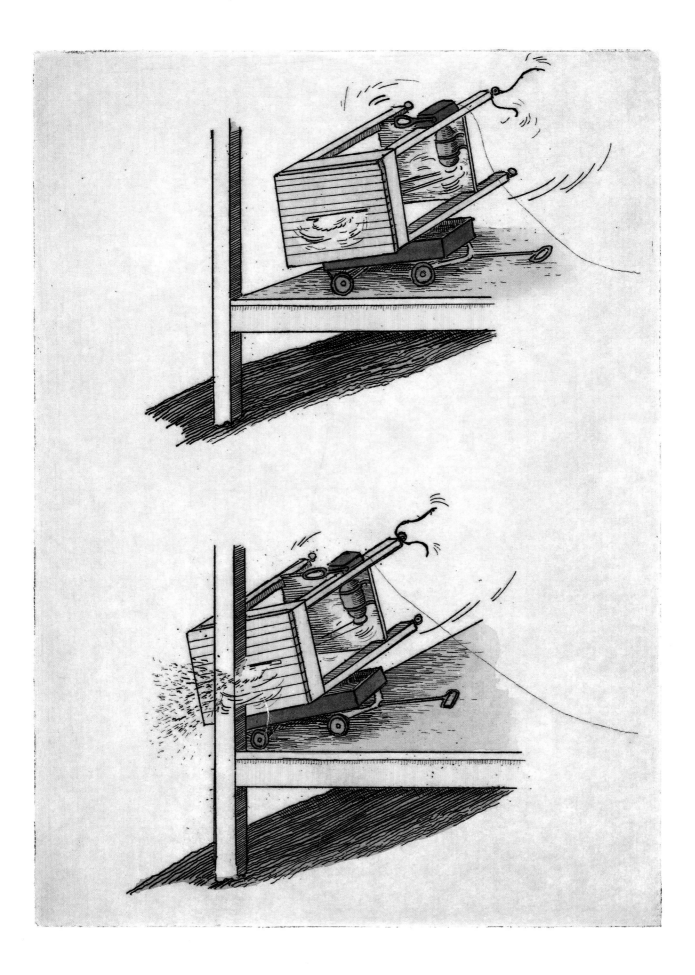

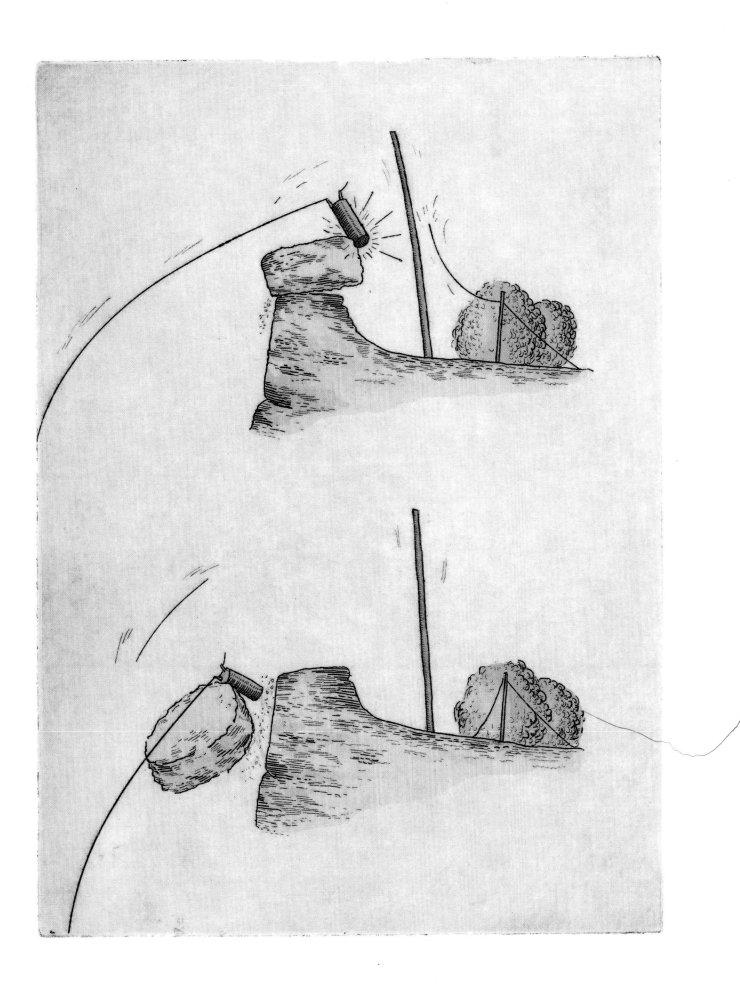